LEARN AND HAVE

ACTIVITY
&
GAME BOOK

Teora

Basic skills for
4-5 year olds

LEARN AND HAVE FUN: ACTIVITY&GAME BOOK.
Basic skills for 4-5 year olds

© 2005, 2004 Teora USA LLC
2 Wisconsin Circle, Suite 870
Chevy Chase, MD 20815
USA
for the English version
Translated by Adriana Bădescu

© Editions CARAMEL S.A.
Otto de Mentockplein 19
1853 Strombeek-Bever – Belgium

079

ISBN 1-59496-031-3
Printed in Romania

10 9 8 7 6 5 4 3 2 1

Connect each animal in the left column to its shadow in the right column.

The little mermaid always swims along the shells to go to her father. Mark the way she must take. You can start from the shell near her tail and continue to jump down a row or diagonally.

Can you circle the numbers
1 - 2 - 3 - 4 - 5 and 6 on this balloon?

It's spring! Circle the two identical pictures in each column.

Circle one of the two identical objects in each box.
If you will look at the symbol by the side of the picture,
you will know which object to circle.

● = above   ⬚ = below

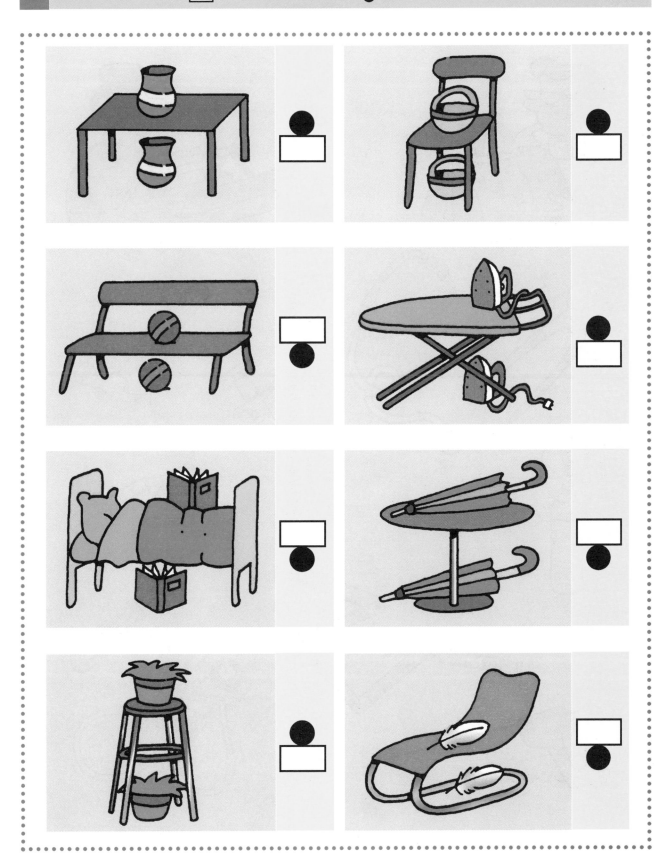

Circle all of the objects that belong in the doctor's case in red. Then circle all of the objects that belong in the worker's case in blue.

Do you recognize the numbers below? Read them aloud and then circle as many objects as each number says.

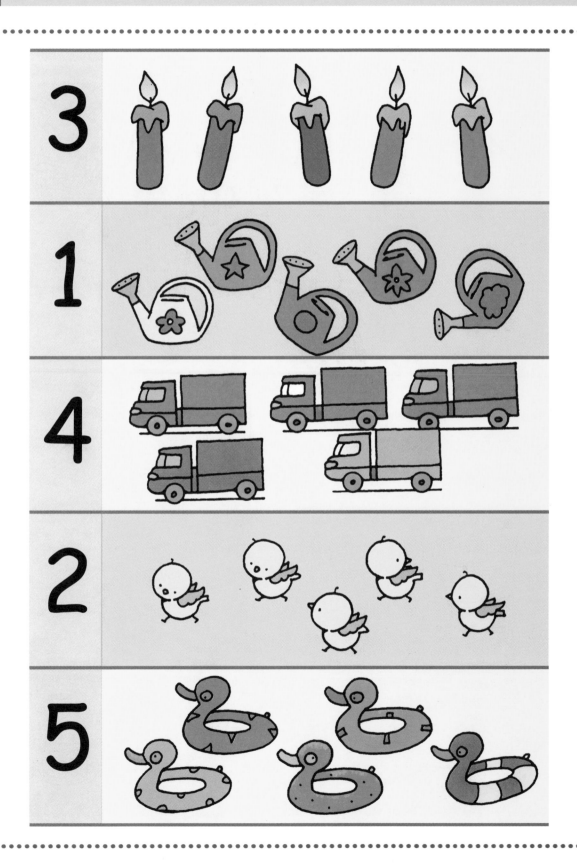

Help mother put the flowers in the right vase. Connect the flowers to the right vase with a red line.

In each row, circle the 2, 3, or 4 objects that have the same length.

Connect the number 5 to all pictures that have 5 parts.

Circle the symbol that corresponds to the large picture.

Connect each circle to a picture in the left column and to another one in the right column. For each circle there are two pictures that match the little object in the circle.

On this page there are 6 pictures with mistakes.
Draw an X on these mistakes.

The king wants to go to his treasure. Help him to find the right way.

This mean thief has robbed two houses.
Circle these two houses.

There are too many trees in this forest.
All of the trees that have a thick trunk must
be cut down. Mark them with an X.

It's summer! In each row, cross out the object that is different.

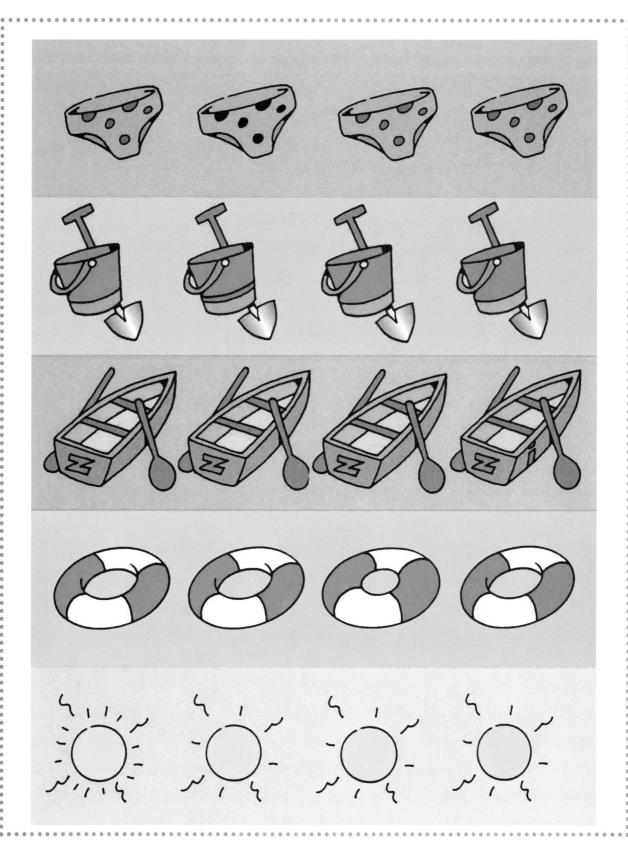

Do you know how to fasten or repair the objects in the right column? Connect the pictures in the left column to the objects they will fix.

Connect each food or drink to the element we can use to eat or drink it.

22

In each row, put the two objects in
the right order. Color in one sun for the first
drawing and two suns for the second one.

Connect each board to the needed number of nails.
To do that, count the holes in each board.

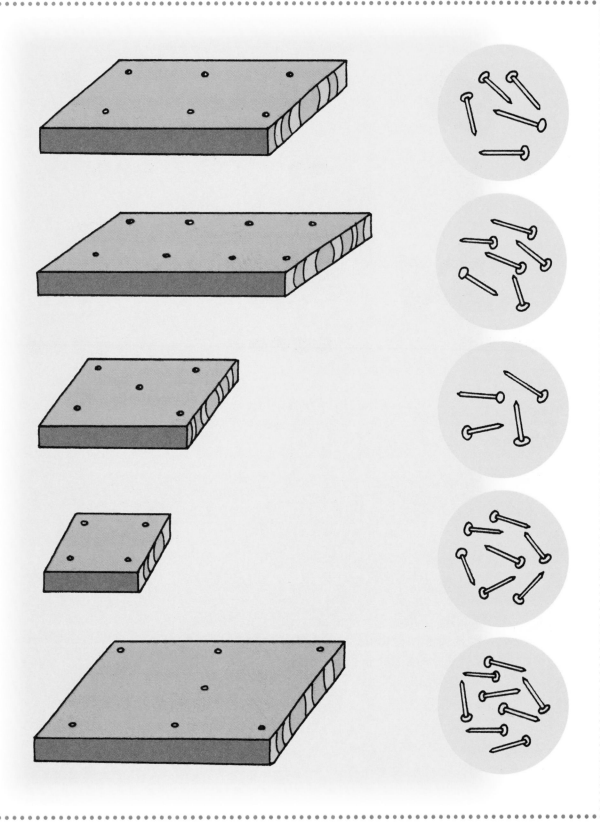

Which pieces in the blue box go with which games in the yellow box? After you have found the answer, color the same number of dots in the yellow box.

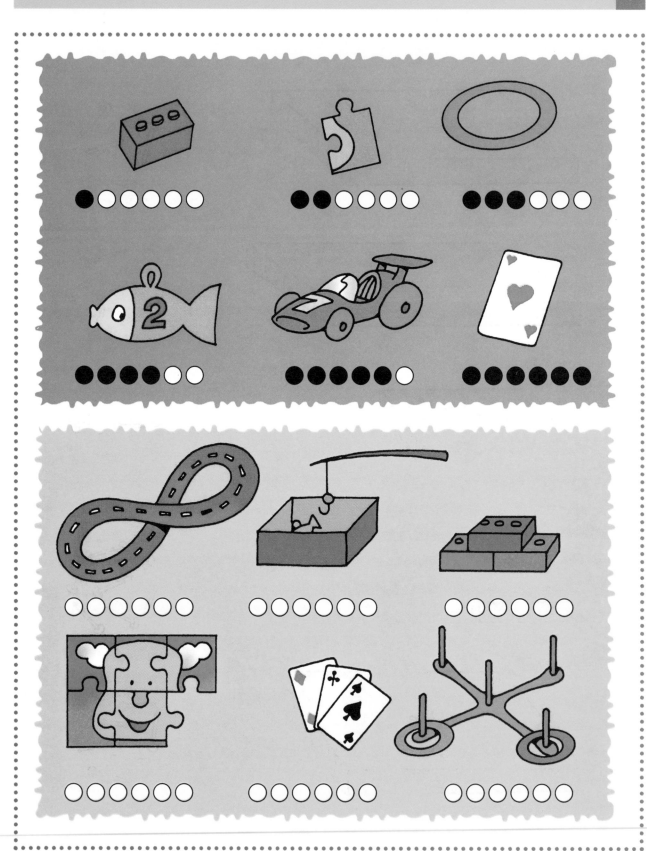

Circle each picture that has one less element than the others in the same row.

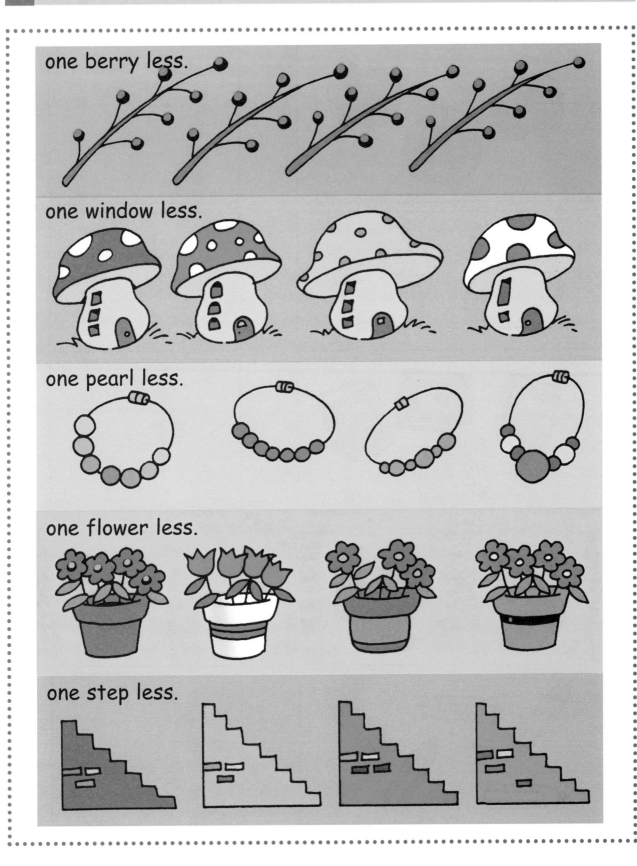

one berry less.

one window less.

one pearl less.

one flower less.

one step less.

Write in the right column the number of objects in the left column.

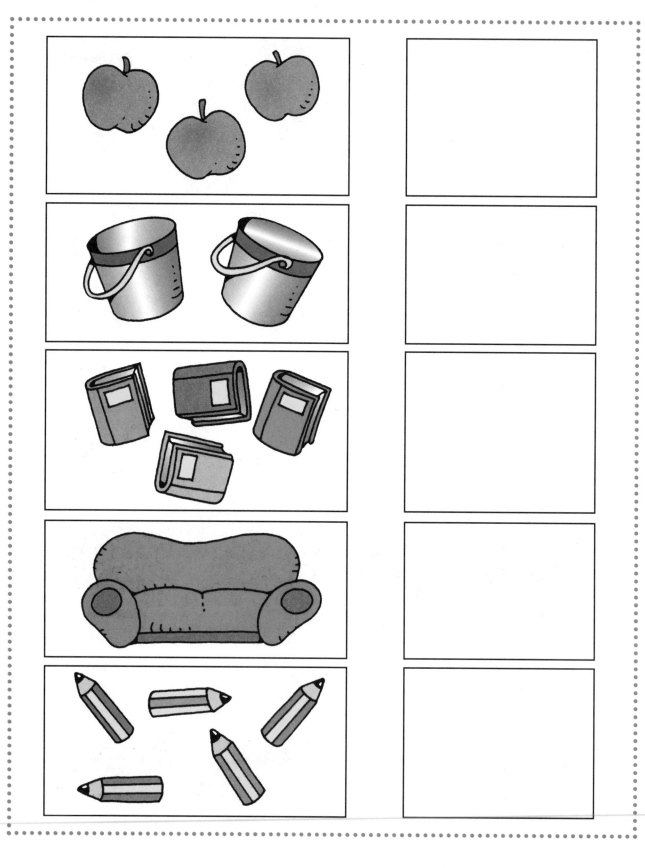

Do you know what is in the trunk? Connect each object in the trunk to the same object outside the trunk. There are two more objects outside than are inside; cross them out.

28 Can you rearrange the pictures of the boys and men
in the Smith family, from the youngest to the oldest one?
For the youngest one, color 1 ❤, for the next one
color 2 ❤, then 3 ❤, and 4 ❤ for the oldest one.

Do the same thing for the girls and women
in the Smith family.

Circle the pictures of mother and father in red.
Circle the pictures of grandma and grandpa in green.

Circle the person or animal that stands right in front of the clown.

The Jones family goes for a walk in the forest.
Connect each person to her or his boots.

Connect each vehicle to the place where it can be found.

In each row there is an object that differs
a little from the others. Circle this object
and add what is missing.

The Smith family just moved to another house.
Help them put the furniture and other
objects in their proper places.
Connect each object to the right room.

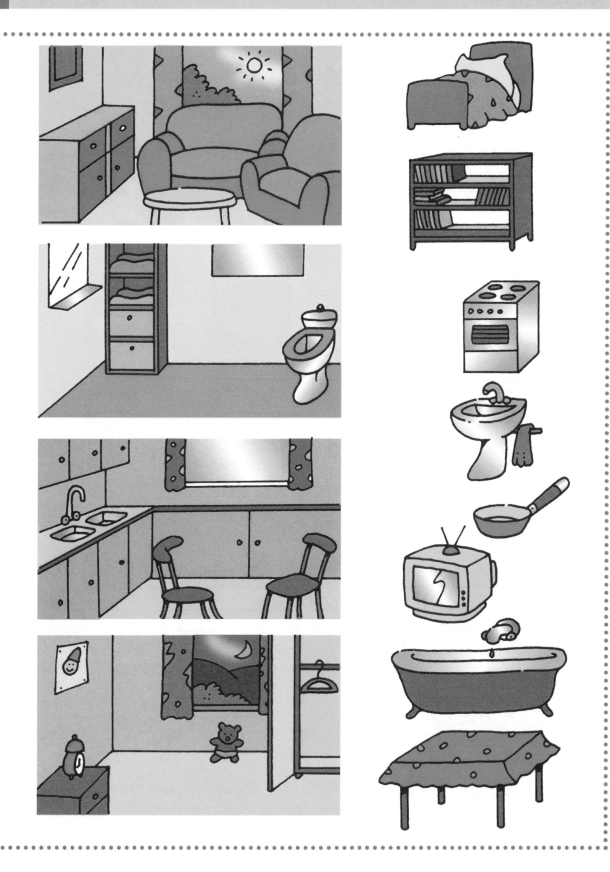

In each row, circle the object that is different.

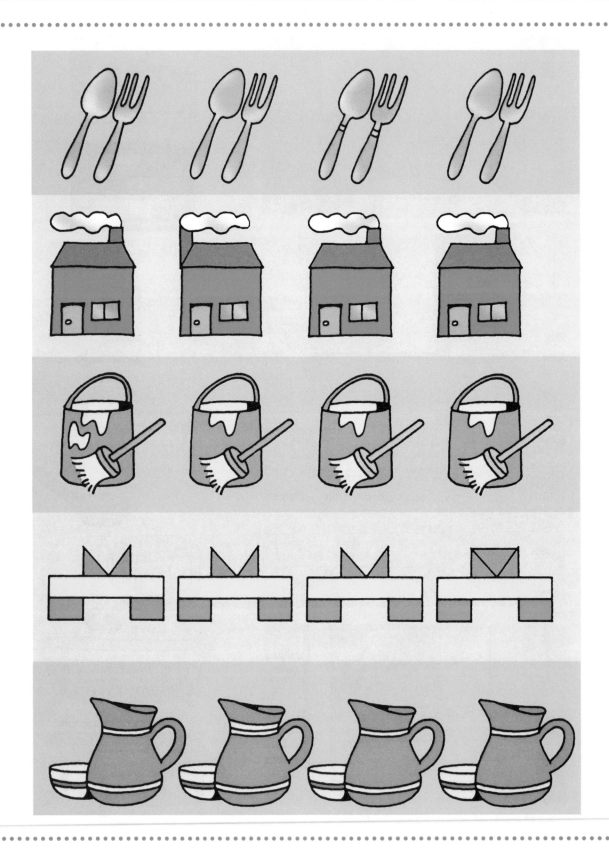

Father needs some objects and tools to work in the garden. Cross out the objects that are not useful to him and circle all of the others.

Read each sentence carefully and circle the correct road sign in red.

1. Pay attention, the train may pass by.

2. The water is not fit to drink.

3. Bicycle riding is not permitted.

4. Pay attention, rocks may fall down.

Circle all objects that are open in red and all
that are closed in blue. Connect each open object
to the same closed object in green.

In each row, circle the vehicle that is like
the one in the yellow column. Pay attention,
the pictures are not identical.

It's autumn! Look on this page for groups of three identical mushrooms and circle them.

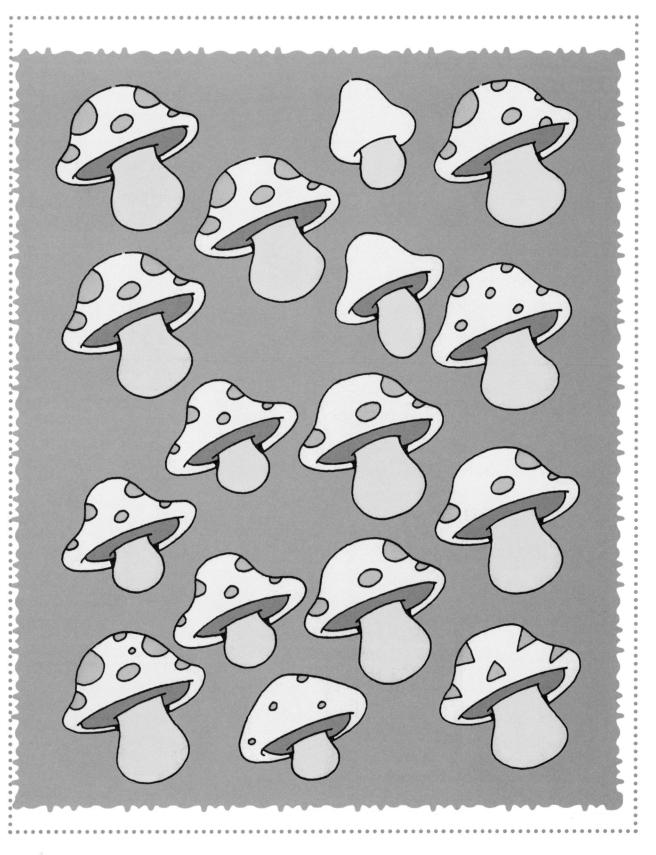

In the left column are only dirty things.
Connect each of these to the object in
the right column that helps to get it clean.

In each row there is one bottle that is different from the other four. Cross it out.

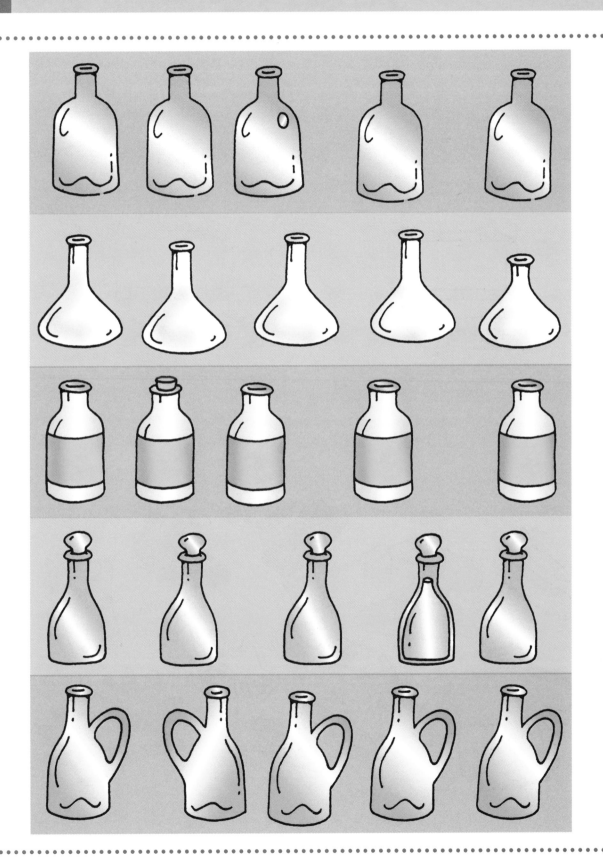

Susie and Ann are setting out on a journey. Susie is going to a warm country and Ann wants to go to a country with cold weather. Help them pack their bags, connecting each object to the right suitcase.

In each box, color in the rectangle under the smallest object.

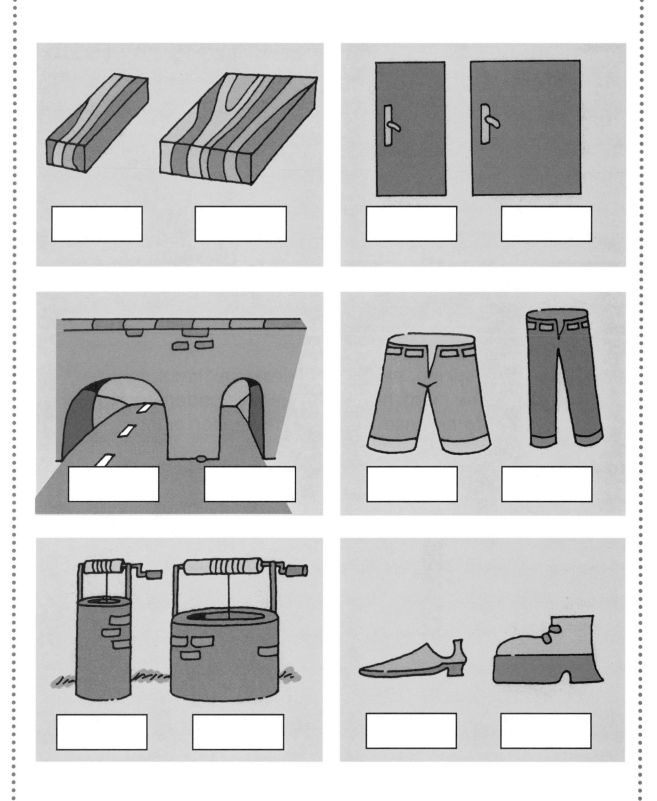

In autumn the leaves fall from the trees.
Decide the order these pictures go in and
color 1 leaf under the first one, 2 leaves under
the second one, and 3 leaves under the third one.

In spring, new leaves grow on trees.
Color the right number of leaves under each
tree to arrange them in the proper order.

Connect the circles that contain the same number of objects.

Circle the objects that do not sound like a ringing bell but are able to play music.

It's winter! In each row there is an object
that has something more than the other three.
Circle this object and cross out the added element.

There is a shelf in the classroom. Find the books that have the same picture on their cover as on the cards hanging on the line. Circle these identical pictures with the same color.

Attention: not every book has a matching card.

Circle the objects that are most like the picture on the left.

Circle the birds that have 6 feathers in their tail.

In each row, circle the object one can see through.

Where do these animals live? Connect each farm animal to its home. Circle all of the forest animals.

Connect the numbers from 1 to 5 in the right order (1 - 2 - 3 - 4 - 5). First connect the numbers that are next to the circles and then the numbers that are next to the triangles.

Do you know which objects are giving light? Circle them.

Connect each picture in the left column to the tool that can cut or remove what needs to be removed.

Mother wants to buy things for her baby.
Circle those objects that are useful for the baby.

Do you recognize the animals that are hiding behind the bushes? Circle those animals at the bottom of the page that you recognize. Put an X on the animal that is found only behind the bushes.

7 dragonflies are flying over the lake. Draw as many lines as necessary for each of them to have 7 stripes.

Do you know which of these objects need water? Circle them.

Connect the boxes that have the same number of balls.

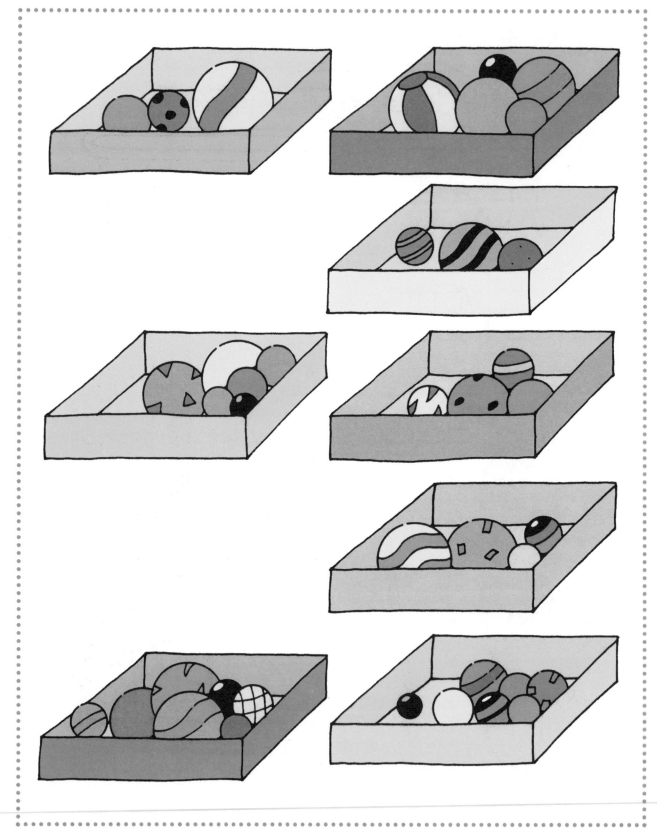

Find out what present these people are about to give to the lady . If you are looking carefully, you will see that a small part of the present can be seen behind each person. Connect each object at the bottom of the page to the person with that present.

In each box, circle the object that does not belong there.

Connect each object to the person it belongs to.

Connect each animal to its favorite food.

There are good elves and bad elves in this forest.
Each elf has its own flag in front of its burrow.
Circle the flags of the good elves in red and
the flags of the bad ones in blue.

In each row, circle as many objects as indicated by the number in the left column.

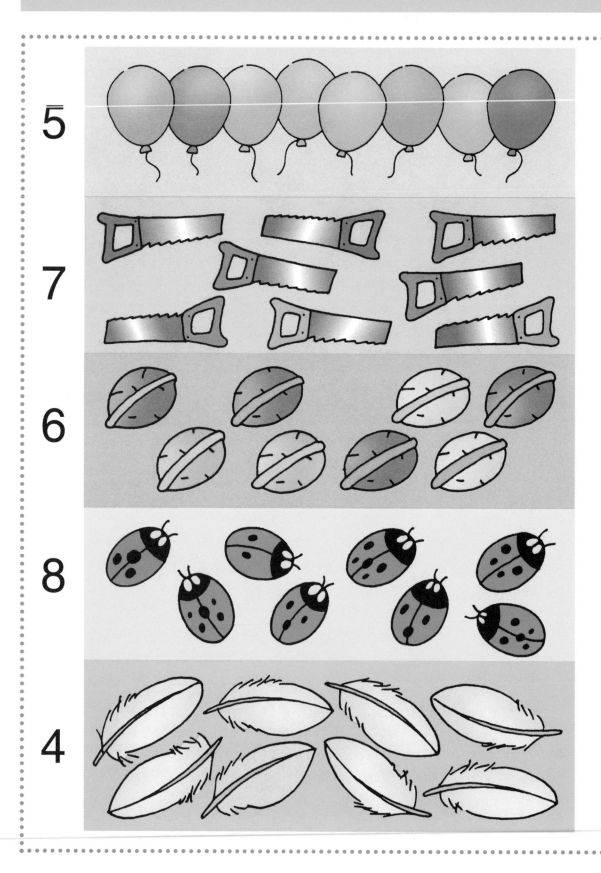

5

7

6

8

4

The giraffe that has the longest neck likes to eat the leaves on the highest branch. The giraffe with the shortest neck can only feed on the lowest branch. Connect each giraffe to its branch.

Look in the house for the objects pictured outside
it and circle the matched pairs with the same color.

Look for the letter A in the picture below.
Circle all of the letters A you can find.

All of these girls are taking part in a swimming contest. Read the numbers on their bathing suits and connect each girl to her diving platform.

In each row there is an object that does not belong there. Cross it out.

In each row, circle the vehicle that runs behind the bicycle.

In each row, color the rectangle under the picture red when the object is completely open. Color the rectangle blue when the object is completely closed.

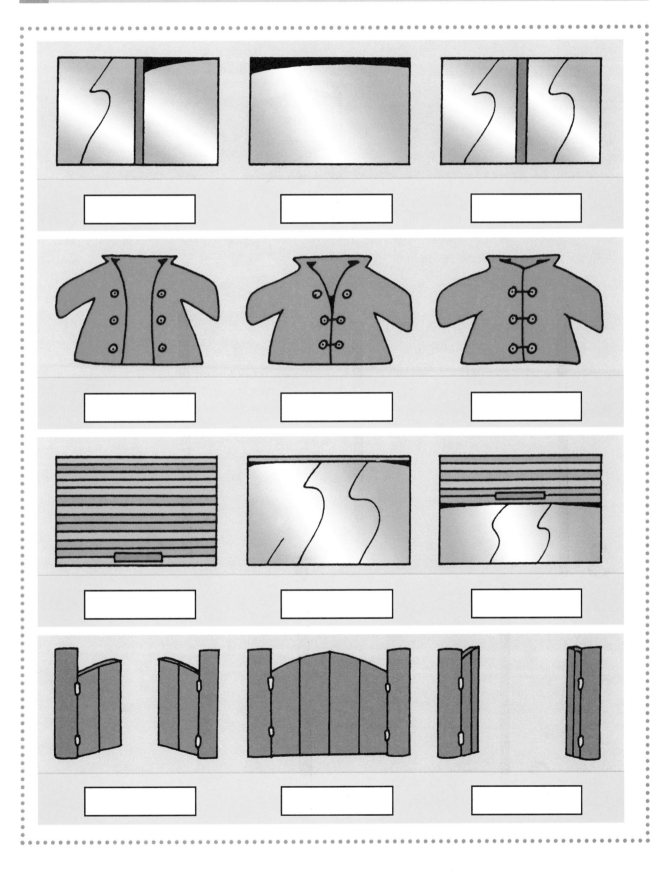

For each pole, draw as many flags as the number indicates.

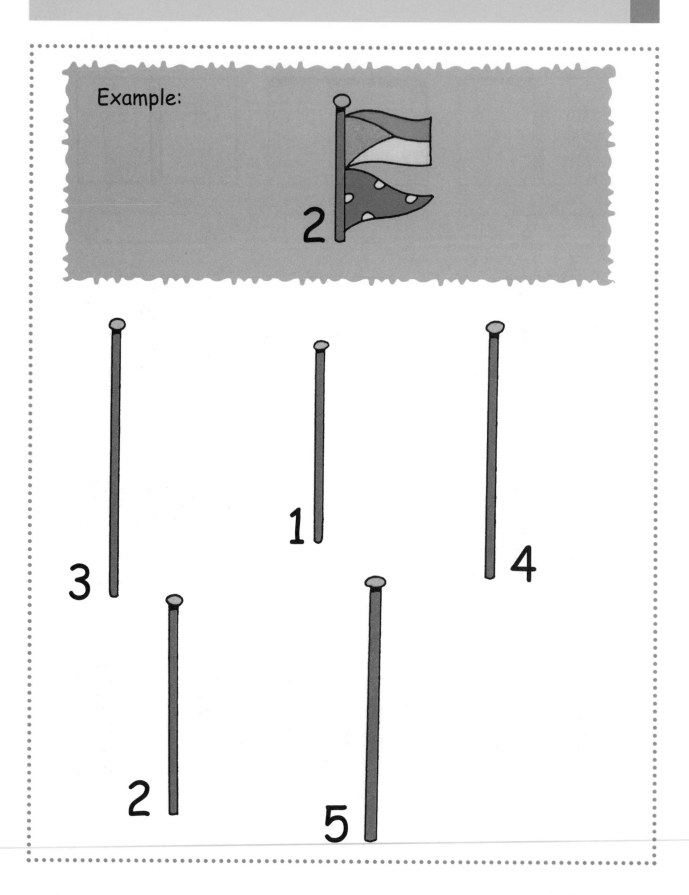

Example:

2

Susie and Ann want to play cards. Each one of them has a card before her and there are 6 more cards to distribute. Draw 1 circle when the card is suitable for Susie and 2 circles when the card is suitable for Ann.

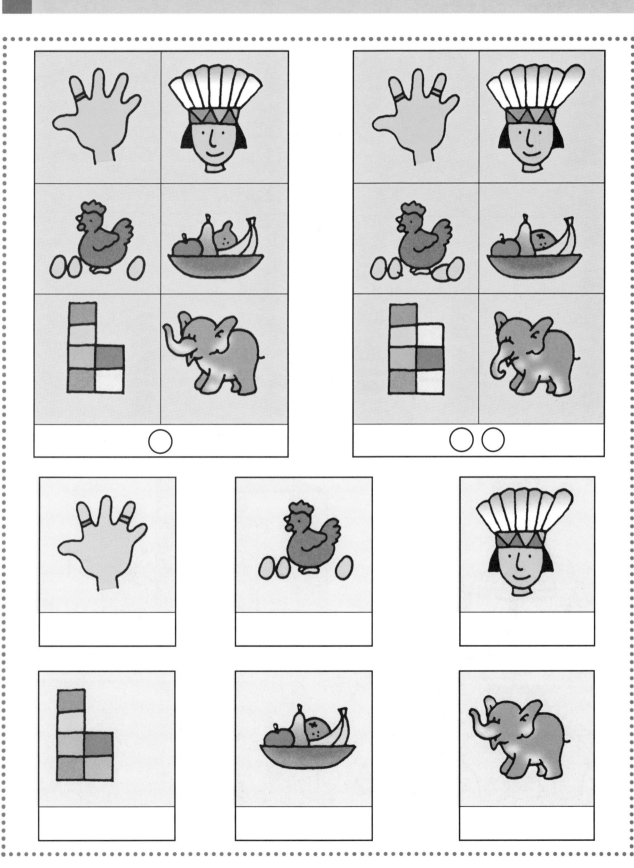

Circle the boys standing between two pieces of furniture.

Which one of the two vehicles that take part in the competition is faster and will win the race? Connect this vehicle to the cup on the same row.

Circle in the large picture the number of objects indicated by the numbers in the smaller boxes.

What is the right order of the 4 following pictures?
Color 1 half moon for the first part of the story,
2 half moons for the second part and so on, up to
4 half moons for the last part of the story.

Circle the 4 animals on whose back a person can ride.

page 3

page 4

page 5

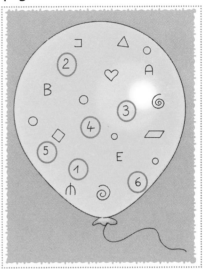

page 6

page 7

page 8

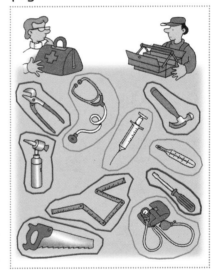

page 9

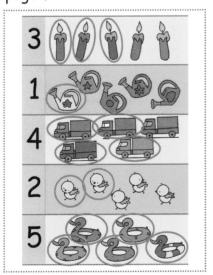

page 10

page 11

page 12

page 13

page 14

page 15

page 16

page 17

page 18

page 19

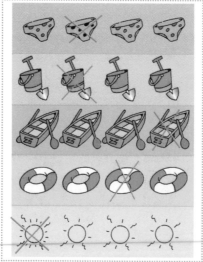

page 20

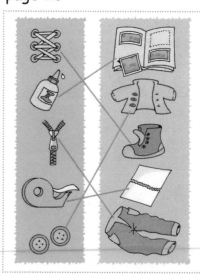

page 21

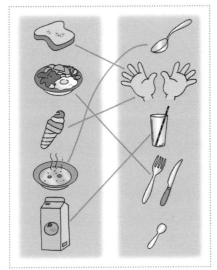

page 22

page 23

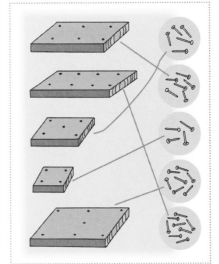

page 24

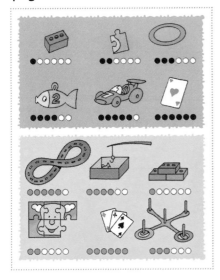

page 25

page 26

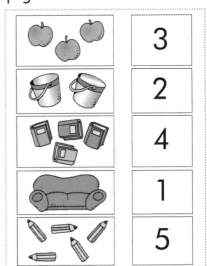

page 27

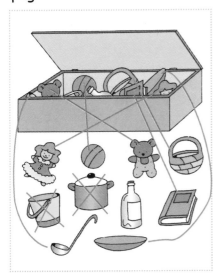

page 28

page 29

page 30

page 31

page 32

page 33

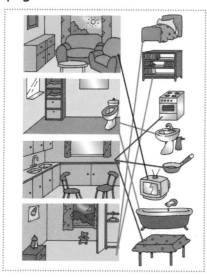

page 34

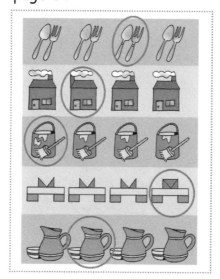

page 35

page 36

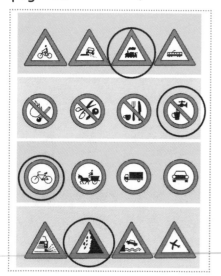

page 37

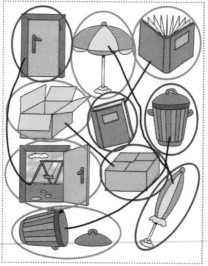

page 38

page 39

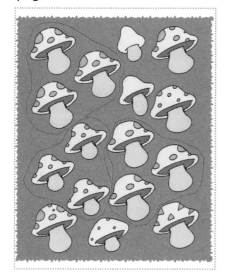

page 40

page 41

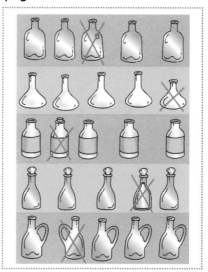

page 42

page 43

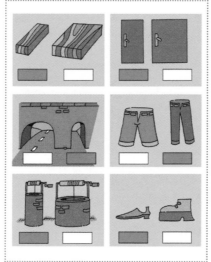

page 44

page 45

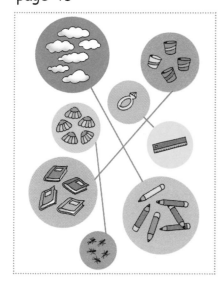

page 46

page 47

page 48

page 49

page 50

page 51

page 52

page 53

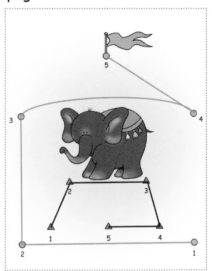

page 54

page 55

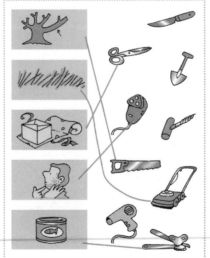

page 56

page 57

page 58

page 59

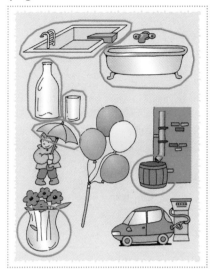

page 60

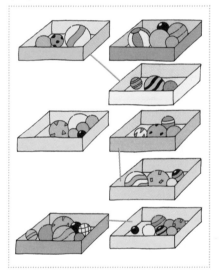

page 61

page 62

page 63

page 64

page 65

page 66

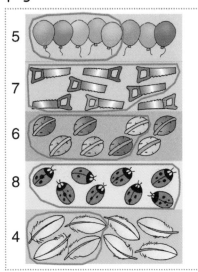

page 67

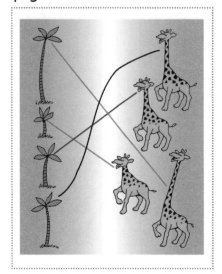

page 68

page 69

page 70

page 71

page 72

page 73

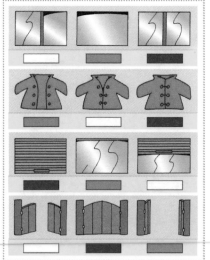

page 74

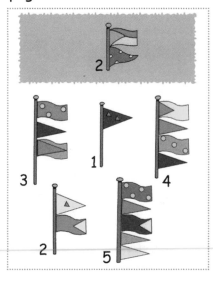

page 75

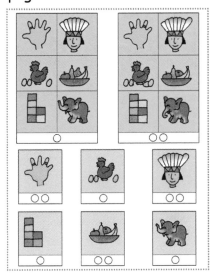

page 76

page 77

page 78

page 79

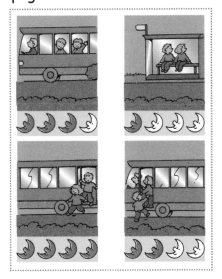

page 80